The Remembering Box

The Remembering Box

Eth Clifford

Illustrated by Donna Diamond

Houghton Mifflin Company
Boston

Library of Congress Cataloging in Publication Data

Clifford, Eth, 1915–
    The remembering box.

    Summary: Nine-year-old Joshua's weekly visits to
his beloved grandmother on the Jewish Sabbath give
him an understanding of love, family, and tradition
which helps him accept her death.
    [1. Grandmothers—Fiction.   2. Jews—Fiction.
3. Death—Fiction]   I. Diamond, Donna, ill.   II. Title.
PZ7.C62214Re   1985   [Fic]   85-10851
ISBN 0-395-38476-1

        Printed in the United States of America

    v   10   9   8   7   6   5

With much love, this book is for my husband
David, for it is as much his as mine.

The Remembering Box

1

Ever since he was five, Joshua Beck had gone to visit his grandmother Goldina on the Sabbath. His father took Joshua to Grandma Goldina's apartment right after school on Friday afternoons. Then he went away and didn't come back until well after dark on Saturday evening.

Joshua really liked his Sabbaths with Grandma Goldina. If a Roy Rogers movie was playing that day, he sometimes wished he could go, but he couldn't do that on the Sabbath anyhow.

Joshua loved Westerns, especially those with Roy Rogers and his wonderful horse Trigger. Roy Rogers sang a lot. When he did, Joshua ran up and down the aisles with the other kids, or changed his seat several times, or clapped his hands noisily and whistled to hurry Roy Rogers to get back to being a cowboy again.

Sometimes Joshua's father didn't let him visit

Grandma Goldina because he had made his father angry. One time Joshua pushed his brother Ari so hard on the rocking chair, the rocker went spinning over, taking Ari with it and giving Ari a bloody nose and a big bump on his head. That time Joshua couldn't see Grandma Goldina for two Sabbaths in a row.

And every once in a while, Joshua just wanted to be home to share Shabbat with his family.

But Grandma Goldina always understood. She was happy to see him when he did come, and would hug him so hard Joshua could hardly breathe.

"Come in! Come in!" Grandma Goldina always greeted Joshua. "Guess what I made for you today."

She made all of Joshua's favorite foods. Sometimes it was blintzes, which were cheese-filled pancakes. She ate them with gobs of sour cream on top, but Joshua liked his blintzes with applesauce. Other times she prepared chopped liver with lots and lots of fried onions, or ice-cold schav, a soup Grandma Goldina made from spinach and leaves from the sorrel plant, which had a delicious sour flavor.

Joshua remembered that when he was little, when he first started going to Grandma Goldina's, they used to play games. One of his favorite games was hide-and-go-seek.

Grandma Goldina was a small woman, but she couldn't hide under the table the way Joshua did when it was his turn. Instead she would stand next

to the icebox and cover her face with her hands.
Then she would call, "Ready!"

Joshua saw her right away, of course, but he always pretended he couldn't find her.

"Where can she be?" he would wonder aloud.

When he finally found her, he would say,
"There you are, Grandma!"

He loved the way she laughed then.

On nice days they went for long walks. At least
they seemed long to Joshua when he was still little.
When he grew bigger, the walks seemed shorter to
Joshua, but somehow they became longer for
Grandma Goldina.

"Can't you walk faster?" Joshua asked one day
when his grandmother slowed down.

"What's my hurry?" she answered calmly.

"When I get there, I'll only have to turn around and come back."

Sometimes Joshua was impatient and raced ahead. Then he would run back and try to match his steps to hers.

When they arrived back at the apartment, Grandma Goldina would say, "It's time for you to rest, Joshua."

They both knew it was Grandma Goldina who needed to rest. She would kick off her heavy walking shoes, sit back on the sofa with a big sigh, and pat the cushion next to her. This was one of the best parts of spending Shabbat with his grandmother. For this was reading time, and story-telling time.

Now that Joshua was nine, he could read very well by himself. But he still liked to curl up next to Grandma Goldina, especially on rainy days. He liked the sound of her voice.

When she grew tired of reading, his grandmother told Joshua stories about a place called "the old country," which was a land far across the sea.

2

Sometimes Grandma Goldina sang to Joshua. Some of the songs were funny and made Joshua laugh. Other songs were sad. Then Joshua would feel sad, too, even though he didn't understand most of the words. For Grandma Goldina often sang these songs in the language of the old country.

Whenever Grandma talked of her life in the old country or sang her sad songs, her voice was low and soft. Her thoughts seemed to be far away. Sometimes tears made her pale blue eyes shiny and bright.

"Don't cry," Joshua begged when this happened. "Please don't cry, Grandma."

Then Grandma dried her eyes with her handkerchief. Smiling, she explained, "These are not my crying tears, Joshua. These are my remembering tears."

That surprised Joshua. "You give names to *tears?*"

Grandma Goldina shrugged. "We have different names for different feelings, yes? So different names for different tears."

"But Grandma," Joshua began to object, "tears are always the same. They just pop into your eyes and roll down . . ." He drew two deep lines down his cheeks with his forefingers to show her.

Grandma Goldina closed her eyes and shook her head vigorously, the way she did when she disagreed with what was being said.

"Outside tears come from inside feelings," Grandma Goldina explained. "So how can they be the same? I'll give you a for instance. You know what happens when I laugh hard? I cry," she went on, without waiting for Joshua to answer. "Right?"

"Right," Joshua agreed. He'd seen Grandma Goldina burst into laughter lots of times. She would grasp her throat, make small choking sounds, reach for a handkerchief, dry her eyes, and blow her nose.

"So what would you call those tears?"

"Happy?" Joshua asked.

"You see?" she said with a triumphant smile. "And when your little brother Daniel was so sick with scarlet fever, and we almost lost him . . ." Grandma Goldina stopped talking. Even now it was hard for her to speak about that time.

Joshua remembered it well. Daniel was only two years old then. Grandma Goldina came to the house

every day to sit by Daniel's side. She would rock back and forth, then turn her head away so Daniel wouldn't see the tears streaming from her eyes.

"Those were sad tears. They were very sad," Joshua said.

"Sad, yes. But it was more. They were my hurting tears." She chucked him under the chin. "There's always a reason for crying."

"Oh no, there isn't." Joshua's eyes grew merry, because now he was going to prove to his grandmother that there wasn't always a reason for crying. "You cry at the movies! Even though it's only a make-believe story!"

"A make-believe story can touch your heart," she told him.

"Then are they make-believe tears?"

Grandma Goldina laughed. "Very good, Joshua. That I never thought of. It's better than my name . . . sympathy tears."

Joshua thought his name was better, too.

Even though his grandmother had carefully explained her different tears, it still made Joshua nervous when she cried. But he never minded her Shabbat tears, because Grandma Goldina's Shabbat tears were special.

Each Friday night, at sundown, Grandma Goldina lit the Sabbath candles. First she covered her head with a lace scarf. Then, before lighting the candles, she would say the blessing in Hebrew. Joshua knew it, too, and recited it along with his

grandmother. And Joshua knew all the English
words for the blessing:

Blessed art Thou, O Lord our G-d,
King of the universe, who hath
sanctified us by His commandments,
and hath commanded us to kindle
the light of the holy Sabbath.
Amen.

When the candles were lit, Grandma Goldina
circled her hands three times over the flame, closed
her eyes, and prayed. After a while she dropped her
hands, opened her eyes, which were always filled
with tears, and said in a happy voice, "Shabbat Shalom, Joshua."

"Shabbat Shalom," Joshua replied.

He had known these words long before he
started spending the Sabbath with his grandmother.
As far back as he could remember, his mother also
lit candles each Friday evening at dusk. Everyone
watched, first Joshua, and then Ari and Daniel
when they came along. And when his little sister
Shoshanah was still a baby, Joshua's mother had let
him hold Shoshanah so she could watch, too. She
would stare unblinkingly as the flames from the
candles flickered, her large brown eyes solemn with
wonder.

When Joshua's mother finally said, "Shabbat
Shalom. Sabbath peace," her eyes were gentle with

love as she looked at her family. Then she kissed everyone.

Then Joshua's father kissed his mother and all the children, starting with Joshua.

Joshua thought about the first time he had seen tears in Grandma Goldina's eyes after the prayer.

"Mommy never cries when she says the blessing. Why are you crying, Grandma?" he wanted to know.

"Crying? This is not crying, Joshua. These are the tears of my soul."

Every Friday night he spent with her after that, Joshua waited for Grandma Goldina's hands to drop, so he could touch her face and brush away the tears of her soul.

3

Joshua had a special reason for liking Grandma Goldina's remembering tears — because they happened when he and Grandma Goldina looked through her remembering box.

The remembering box wasn't really a box at all, but a trunk with two long straps around it, and a lock that didn't work. It was full of all kinds of things.

Each Saturday afternoon Joshua dipped his hand into the trunk and pulled something out. Then his grandmother would study whatever it was and tell Joshua a story about it.

Once Joshua pulled out a branch shaped something like the letter *Y*.

"What a funny stick," Joshua said, turning it round and round. "How come you saved this old stick anyway?"

Grandma Goldina reached over and took it away. Her eyes had that faraway look.

"This funny stick came from a willow tree near our house in the old country. My grandfather Schmuel used this stick to find water in the ground."

"What for?" Joshua wondered.

"If he found water, then he knew where to dig a well. We didn't have water in the house. Nobody did. We got our water from a well."

Joshua settled back to listen to a new story about the old country.

"My grandfather was a giant of a man," Grandma Goldina said. "When he walked, the earth shook. When he laughed, the birds fell out of the trees. His hair caught fire from the sun. His eyes were patches of sky."

Joshua grinned. Grandma Goldina told stories as if she were writing a book.

Joshua had red hair and blue eyes like Grandma Goldina's grandfather. But the earth didn't shake when Joshua walked. And birds were safe in the trees when Joshua laughed.

"When someone wanted to dig a well," his grandmother continued, "they called my grandfather Schmuel, the water finder. He would come with his willow branch and walk back and forth across the land, holding the branch out in front of him, moving it slowly, slowly, slowly."

Grandma Goldina stood up to show Joshua how

Schmuel the water finder searched the land. She took a few steps at a time, all the while staring down intently.

Suddenly her hands trembled. The stick pointed down sharply toward the floor.

"Water!" Grandma Goldina shouted. *"Water!"*

Joshua knew there really wasn't any water there, but his grandmother acted the part so well! Besides, Joshua liked to play-act, too. So he knelt down, patted the carpet, and pretended that it was wet.

Then he looked up at Grandma Goldina with a big smile.

"I can find water. You want to see?" he asked.

When she nodded, he went into the kitchen and turned on the tap. Water came pouring out into the sink.

"And I didn't need a stick to find it," Joshua said.

But later, when they went out for their walk, Joshua took the willow branch along. While his grandmother stayed on the sidewalk, Joshua went back and forth over the grass.

He found water, too, just like Schmuel the water finder. But Joshua's water came from a sprinkler someone hadn't turned off all the way, making a puddle at the curb, in which a bird was busily taking a bath.

"See?" Joshua teased. "I'm just like your grand-father Schmuel."

"I see," she said. "Another miracle worker.

Come, my big water finder. I'll make you something special today."

When they returned to Grandma Goldina's apartment, she put the branch carefully into the remembering box, even though Joshua wanted to keep it.

"Not yet," she told him. Then she sighed. "My wonderful grandfather."

She stared into space, and remembering tears washed her eyes.

4

Joshua was amazed at how many pictures he found in the remembering box. He liked to sort through them, especially on rainy days, or chilly days, when the sky was gray and people rushed past his grandmother's window with their heads down and their shoulders hunched against the cold.

Most of the people in the pictures stared straight out at Joshua, with dark, serious eyes and a pinched tight look around their mouths.

Everyone wore strange clothes. The men's suits were black; their oddly shaped hats were black. Even their beards and mustaches and sideburns were black.

The women wore dresses so long their shoes were hidden. The collars were high around their necks, and their sleeves came all the way down to their wrists.

Some of the women wore large hats. Grandma Goldina explained that they were kept in place on the women's heads with hatpins.

She found two hatpins in the remembering box. The pins looked like long, wicked needles, with pearls on one end and sharp points on the other.

"Didn't they hurt?" Joshua asked.

"You think they stuck the pins through their heads?" Grandma Goldina asked. "The pins went through the hat and through the hair. I had a lot of hair in those days," she added thoughtfully.

Joshua stared at his grandmother's hair, lying wispy and thin, her pink scalp peeking through. It was hard for him to imagine she ever had enough hair in which to stick a hatpin.

"How come nobody ever smiled?" Joshua wanted to know.

His mother had boxes of pictures on a shelf in the hall closet. Some were marked *Joshua, Ari, Daniel, Shoshanah,* while others just had *Family* on the covers.

Joshua's mother had once started to put all the pictures neatly in photograph albums, with names and dates written carefully on each page. But after Ari was born, she postponed that task until later, except that later never seemed to come around.

One thing Joshua knew, however. In all the pictures in all the boxes, everyone smiled and smiled.

"In the old days it was different. It wasn't like today," his grandmother explained. "Having your picture taken was hard work. You had to sit still and not move, sometimes not even breathe, until the photographer got you fixed the way he wanted you. You had to go to his studio. It could be a day's trip. And you only had your picture taken once. So it was a very serious business for everybody."

Joshua had been sorting through the pictures quickly while his grandmother talked. Now he showed her a picture of a twelve-year-old girl, her hair braided and tied with ribbons, wearing a grin so broad dimples showed in her cheeks.

"Who's this? How come *she's* laughing?"

Grandma Goldina studied the picture and sighed. "The photographer looked so funny I had to laugh. He was like a little rooster crowing at everybody. My poor Mama was embarrassed and my Papa didn't talk to me all the way home."

"This was *you?*" Joshua stared at the smiling girl and then at his grandmother.

"Your face was so different," he said.

The girl had smooth, fair skin. Grandma Goldina's face was covered with tiny wrinkles.

"I used that face up in seventy-five years," she said.

Joshua ran his hand over his own face. "Will I use mine up, too?"

"I hope so, because I want you to live a long, long time."

"Like you, Grandma?"

She nodded. "Like me. Only better."

"Where are all these people now?" Joshua asked.

Grandma Goldina looked away. She was quiet for a minute. Then she said one word, "Gone."

Joshua knew what the word meant, but he didn't feel anything. His grandfather Abba — Grandma Goldina's husband — had died long before Joshua was born. And the other people in the pictures didn't seem real to him. Yet his grandmother looked so sad.

He wanted to see her eyes light up again. So he went back to the picture of the twelve-year-old smiling girl.

"Shoshanah has ribbons like that," he pointed out.

"Of course she has ribbons," Grandma Goldina said promptly. "Why wouldn't she? Isn't she my granddaughter, after all? Let me tell you a story," she continued, and the smile was back in her eyes.

5

Grandma Goldina reached into the remembering box. Joshua was disappointed when he saw what she pulled out.

"*Ribbons?* You're going to tell me a story about *ribbons?* I'm a boy, Grandma. Boys don't care about ribbons."

"But boys like horses, right? Like a horse called Trigger, maybe? Shhh." She held up a warning finger to keep him from talking. "All my life I loved ribbons," she began. "When I was a little girl, I tied ribbons on the rag dolls my Mama made for me. I wouldn't touch my breakfast until she put ribbons on my braids."

Grandma Goldina emptied the bag of ribbons she had taken from the remembering box and let them fall all over the sofa and Joshua and the floor.

Joshua's eyes widened. He'd never seen so many ribbons — wide ones, narrow ones, short ones, long ones — red, green, yellow, blue, white, every color Joshua could name.

What's more, Grandma Goldina knew exactly when she had gotten each ribbon. Here were the ones from flowers Grandpa Abba had given her on birthdays and anniversaries. Over here were ribbons from caps she had knitted for Joshua's brothers Ari and Daniel and for his sister Shoshanah when they were babies.

"What about me?" Joshua demanded. "Didn't you make anything for me when I was little?"

"What a question!" She reached down to pick up a small package that had fallen near the sofa. Joshua read the words Grandma Goldina had written on it in small, crowded letters, *Joshua, the first born, June 1, 1933.*

"You've kept my ribbons nine years!" Joshua exclaimed. He didn't know why he was so pleased. He didn't even like ribbons!

"I'm a saving woman," she told him. "Here. Look at this."

Grandma Goldina showed Joshua two ribbons so faded it was hard to believe they were once bright blue, as she claimed.

"These I used to tie on my horse," she told him.

"You had a horse?" Joshua exclaimed.

"Of course a horse. What's the big surprise? When I was a girl, who knew about cars?"

"Your *own* horse?"

"Well, not exactly."

22

"How can you not exactly have a horse, Grandma? That's silly."

"So if you'll wait, I'll tell you. You see, my father was a horse trader —"

"Just like in the movie I saw last week," Joshua interrupted. "There was this bad guy, see? He said he was a horse trader, but he really stole horses, and Roy Rogers —"

"Wait! Stop! Enough with your Roy Rogers. That's another *not exactly*." She pointed to a stiffly posed man in one of the pictures. "This was my father. He looks to you like one of your bad guy cowboys?"

Joshua couldn't help teasing his grandmother. He pressed his lips together, frowned, and squinted at the picture. Then he said, "Well, not exactly."

"You want to hear this story, Mr. Funny Man?" she asked. When Joshua nodded, she went on. "It was the way my father made his living. To him, a horse was just a horse. But to me . . ." She waved her hands to show how she felt about horses. "One day he brought home a real beauty. He had a shining coat the color of the wild chestnuts I used to pick from the ground when they fell from the chestnut tree. Red and brown. Even his eyes were red-brown."

Joshua kept his glance fixed on his grandmother's face. She seemed to be moving away from him, back into the long ago.

"He was a riding horse. The people my father

23

sold horses to wanted big, heavy work animals. So my father let me take care of this one horse until he could go to a big town to sell him."

"Did he have a name?" Joshua asked.

"Mazel."

"Mazel?" Joshua tried to hide his disappointment. Trigger was a much better name for a horse. Probably there never was a horse in any Western called Mazel!

Grandma Goldina's eyes twinkled. "Could you expect a better name from a girl who wore ribbons? Listen. I called him Mazel because he was my good luck. Mazel was my first love. When I felt sad or lonely or upset, I used to go and talk to Mazel. He knew what I was saying. He would nuzzle me with his soft nose, and I would put my arms around his neck.

"I wasn't supposed to ride him," Grandma Goldina said dreamily. "But sometimes I would jump on his back . . . bareback, no saddle." She leaned forward and whispered, as if it were still a secret she had to keep. "And I didn't sit sideways, the way a girl was supposed to sit on a horse in those days. Together we would ride like the wind down the road and through the woods."

"Did your father get mad at you?"

"Whenever he found out," Grandma Goldina admitted. "But I couldn't help it. When Mazel and I sailed over fences or bushes, we were in a different world, just the two of us."

Joshua closed his eyes, trying to imagine his grandmother as a young girl racing across the land on a swift red-brown horse. When he opened his eyes, she was putting the ribbons back in her ribbon bag.

"Blue ribbons for me, blue ribbons for Mazel," Grandma Goldina said in a low voice.

The horse must have been beautiful. Joshua could tell from the way his grandmother spoke Mazel's name. He sighed.

The nearest he'd ever come to a horse was when his father took him and Ari to Central Park for a ride on a pony. But a man had held Joshua and then Ari in the saddle, and the pony had just plodded round and round a dirt track.

"It's too bad you don't have a picture of Mazel," Joshua began, then stopped when his grandmother started to laugh.

"Of course! What I should have done was bring Mazel to the studio. I can just see that photographer's face. Never mind that. I can just see my *father's* expression!"

Joshua couldn't help laughing, too. Wouldn't all those stiffly posed people have stared!

"Someday I'll have my own horse, just like you, Grandma." When he owned a horse, he would ride like the wind down long country roads and through the woods, too.

"Can I have this picture of you?" he asked suddenly.

Grandma Goldina took it from his hand. She put it back carefully into the remembering box along with the other pictures.

"Not now, Joshua," she said quietly. "Not yet."

6

Joshua knew his father and mother had tried to get Grandma Goldina to move in with them. They started talking to her about it when Joshua was five. But his grandmother always refused.

She made lots of excuses. Their small apartment wasn't big enough for one more person. She loved the children, but four little ones all day long at her age? And two women in one kitchen? Grandma Goldina would raise her eyes toward the ceiling and hold up her hands in horror. It would never work.

Each time they insisted, she had another reason. The truth was she liked sleeping in her own bed, working in her own kitchen, and sitting in the quiet of her own living room.

Joshua's parents worried, but they couldn't change Grandma Goldina's mind.

Joshua listened to them talking, saw how serious his father's dark eyes were, how his eyebrows

pulled together in a thick black line across his forehead, and how he ran his hand through his straight, dark hair the way he always did when he was upset.

And Joshua noticed that his mother's light brown eyes lost their merry look, that her wide smiling mouth took on a pinched, sad expression, and that she twisted a single curl of her sandy brown hair around and around, the way she always did when she was upset.

"We've got to do *something*," Joshua's father had said. "I'm concerned about her living alone."

"But what?" his mother had asked.

"I could stay with Grandma," Joshua had announced. "I can take care of her. Then she won't be alone. After all, I'm five now."

His parents had stared at him. They didn't laugh or tell him he was too little.

"You think he could go just for Shabbat?" Joshua's father had asked after a long silence.

"It would be good for both of them," his mother had agreed.

So his father had brought Joshua to Grandma Goldina's house the following Friday afternoon.

"I'm here to protect you, Grandma," Joshua had announced.

"Hoo-hoo!"

Grandma Goldina only said hoo-hoo when she was very impressed.

"You're going to be my big protector?"

"And I'm going to take care of you, too," Joshua had added.

"So who could ask for anything more?" She turned to Joshua's father and waved him away. "Go, Joseph," she told him. "We don't need you anymore."

And that was how Joshua began spending so many Shabbats with Grandma Goldina.

7

Joshua enjoyed preparing for the Sabbath with Grandma Goldina, and he enjoyed it even more as he grew older.

While Grandma Goldina kneaded the dough for the challah, the large braided bread that would soon come out of the oven fragrant and golden, Joshua polished the candlesticks.

Joshua knew exactly what to do. He took the silver polish from the shelf that held the cleaning supplies. He chose soft, clean rags from the rag bag. And he always remembered to spread newspapers on the table.

When Grandma Goldina placed the two large silver candlesticks in front of Joshua, she usually said the same thing.

"Be careful, Joshua. My grandfather Shimon made these candlesticks."

Joshua nodded. He knew all about Grandfather Shimon from Grandma Goldina's stories of the old country. This grandfather was not a bit like Schmuel the water finder, who walked the earth like a giant.

"Nobody ever had two such different grandfathers," Grandma Goldina said.

Joshua began to rub polish on one of the candlesticks, stopping once in a while to inspect his work.

Grandma Goldina leaned over to examine the candlesticks. "You missed a spot here," she pointed out and sat down at the table, though she had work to do. She found it easier to talk this way.

"My grandfather Shimon was small, a real featherweight, with a head too big for his body. I remember he always seemed to keep his head down when anybody talked to him, but he would look up quickly if he thought nobody was watching. Such big, beautiful brown eyes that man had."

"And he had big hands." Joshua stopped polishing to rest a moment. He stared at his own hands. They were big for his size and age. Maybe he would be like Shimon someday. Maybe he would make beautiful things for his grandchildren. He'd made bookends for his mother in the workshop in school; he'd even varnished them before he'd brought them home and proudly given them to her. They looked lopsided to Joshua; just the same, his mother put books between them right away, but not in the living room.

"Big hands?" Grandma Goldina exclaimed. "Clever hands. Golden hands! He could make carvings so fine you couldn't believe human fingers had made them. That he did for his own enjoyment. Candlesticks he made for a living."

Joshua loved these candlesticks. The bases were round and smooth, but the silver rose like tree trunks, twisting and turning up to the leaf-shaped candle holders.

Grandma Goldina had her remembering look.

"He made these for his wife Hannah. When my grandmother Hannah died, she left the candlesticks to my mother. And she left them to me."

"And when I grow up and get married," Joshua put in helpfully, since he had heard this many times before, "my wife will light Shabbat candles in these candlesticks, right?"

"Right. One hundred percent right," Grandma Goldina agreed. "But don't be in a hurry. Take time to be a boy yet."

"Suppose I don't get married?"

Grandma Goldina caught her face between her hands and gasped.

"Not get married? Then how can I dance at your wedding? Don't you want me to dance at your wedding?"

Grandma Goldina stood and put her hands on

her hips. She stamped her feet, turning this way and that. Joshua clapped his hands, keeping time with the steps Grandma Goldina was making up to some tune only she could hear.

Finally she stopped, leaning against a chair.

"Once I could dance a whole night. I was so light, like a feather! I could dance on eggshells and not crack them. But now . . . a few steps and I'm dizzy." She reached over and patted Joshua's cheek. "When you get married, I'll buy a beautiful new dress—"

"And wear ribbons in your hair," Joshua reminded her.

"What else? Of course ribbons in my hair."

Now she glanced down at the old-fashioned watch, which hung from a black ribbon around her neck.

"We're talking, and time is flying. Quick, we have to set the table."

8

During the week, Grandma Goldina ate at a small table in her tiny kitchen. But Shabbat was special.

Joshua helped his grandmother open the bridge table she kept in a closet all week. Then they set it up in the living room. While Grandma Goldina spread the table with a snow white cloth, Joshua brought in the polished silverware and dishes, carefully placing the knives and spoons on the right and the forks on the left of each place setting, just as Grandma Goldina had taught him.

Meanwhile, in the kitchen, Grandma Goldina stirred food in the pots, peeked into the oven, took relishes out of the icebox.

Everything had to be finished before sundown.

"So. We're ready," Grandma Goldina said at last. "Did you wash your hands?"

Joshua nodded. He watched his grandmother

place the candlesticks in the center of the small table. She covered her head with her lace scarf, and recited the blessing over the candles. At last she struck a match along the side of the matchbox, waited until the small flame leaped at the end of the match, and lit the candles.

Grandfather Shimon's candlesticks gleamed. Joshua was proud that he had made them shine.

Grandma Goldina's tears made her eyes glow in the flickering light. But her smile was warm, and her voice was filled with love as she said, "Shabbat Shalom, Joshua."

"Shabbat Shalom," Joshua repeated.

She kissed him, then went into the kitchen to get the food.

Joshua sat back and waited. He looked at the candlesticks again, at the sweet-smelling challah wrapped in a white cloth napkin, at the small piece of gefilte fish with the touch of fiery red horseradish beside it, at another dish with chopped liver shaped into a small mound.

Friday night was the best night of the week. It was always the same, never different, and it was beautiful.

Joshua sighed contentedly and waited for Grandma Goldina to come and sit down so the Shabbat meal could begin.

9

"Grandma," Joshua said, after she had given him a bowl of her homemade chicken soup with *mandlin,* a soup nut that looked like puff pastry but was deliciously crunchy. "You made *mandlin* for me again, so you love me best, right? You love me more than Ari and Shoshanah and Daniel?"

Grandma Goldina shook her head. "I love you, but not best, because I love all my grandchildren. I just love you all for different reasons."

"But you loved me first," Joshua insisted. "Because I came first."

"You came first," Grandma Goldina agreed.

"And I've been taking care of you since I was five years old," he reminded her.

"And now you are nine and you are still taking care of me."

"Do you remember how I used to bring you the

39

pictures I made in kindergarten, and you used to hang them up on the icebox?"

"How could I not remember?" she asked. "I still have them —"

"You *saved* them?" Joshua interrupted. "But Grandma! That was baby stuff. I couldn't even draw!"

"I told you I'm a saving woman —"

Joshua began to laugh. "Do you remember how disappointed I was when you didn't know what I drew?"

Grandma Goldina nodded, grinning. "You handed me a piece of paper and you told me it was a bird sitting in a tree watching a cat on the ground. You were so surprised you had to explain to me what it was supposed to be."

"And one time I made a picture of you, and you looked and looked at it, then you said, 'This is *me*? This is how I look?' and I said, 'Can't you see that it says Grandma?' "

The grandmother on Joshua's paper had a large, round head. Two small dots with circles around them were her eyes. The nose was so long there wasn't room for a mouth.

Long skinny arms dangled from each side of her head. On top of her head were four thin lines that stood straight up, then fell over.

"Because you don't have real hair like me," Joshua had explained.

"Thank you," his grandmother had said. "Well, at least you gave me four hairs and not three."

"How many *do* you have, Grandma?"

"We'll count some other time," she answered.

In the picture, her body started at her chin, going down in a straight line, to which Joshua had added long, skinny legs with tiny feet.

"You like it?" he had asked anxiously.

"What's not to like? It's even better than the bird in the tree watching the cat."

Grandma Goldina had hung the pictures side by side on the icebox door.

"Do you remember when I was in first grade?" Joshua now asked.

His grandmother had removed the soup bowls. From the kitchen, she called back, "I remember."

When Joshua was in the first grade, he didn't draw many pictures. Instead he liked writing. It took him a long time to shape the ABC's. Some went over the lines on the page, some went under. Often he wrote the *B*s and *D*s backward. But after a while he could write words, and then whole sentences.

Joshua was smiling when his grandmother came back into the room with two plates heaped with roast chicken, *kasha varnishkes,* and carrots.

"What's with the smiling?" she asked. "You thought of something funny?"

"Yeah. Me. In first grade. I thought writing was

so hard . . ." Joshua glanced over his shoulder at something hanging on the wall. "How long are you going to keep that?" he asked.

"Forever. In the whole world, nobody ever wrote me such a beautiful letter."

Grandma Goldina reached over and took Joshua's hand in hers.

"Beautiful," she repeated.

"You came to our house and you were crying because your friend died."

"My dear friend, Mrs. Schorr."

"And then I wrote you a letter. I wrote it all by myself. Nobody told me to," Joshua said. "I wanted to."

"I know."

This boy is sad. He is sad because you are sad. Don't be sad, Grandma. I will be your freind. I love you.
Joshua

Grandma Goldina got up to look at the framed letter on the living room wall. Joshua came with her.

Joshua had drawn a picture of a boy with a teardrop falling from each dot of an eye. Next to it he had written: "This boy is sad. He is sad because you are sad. Don't be sad, Grandma. I will be your freind. I love you. Joshua."

The letters were crooked and took up most of the page.

Joshua frowned. "I didn't even spell *friend* right."

Grandma Goldina hugged him. "What's the difference? I knew what you were saying."

She put her arm around his shoulder. "Come," she said. "Supper is getting cold."

10

The next morning, clouds hid the sun. They spun up from the horizon in dark, swirling circles. Now and then lightning flashed in quick, downward streaks.

Joshua counted when he saw the lightning. "One. Two. Three. Four. Five. Six." When he heard the thunder, he nodded.

He had learned in school that light traveled faster than sound. Sound, his teacher said, travels one mile in five seconds, but light travels thousands of miles per second. That was why he saw the lightning first. When he counted from the flash of light to the explosion of thunder, he would know how far away the storm was.

Grandma Goldina didn't know anything about science. But she was the one who had first told Joshua to count. She wasn't the least bit afraid.

When Joshua was very little, thunderstorms had

terrified him. He would hide in a closet with his hands over his ears and his eyes squeezed shut. He wouldn't come out no matter how much his mother or father coaxed him. But the first time it had stormed when he was with his grandmother, she wouldn't let him hide.

"That closet is so small," she told him, "even a fly wouldn't have room in there. Come with me. I'll take care of you."

She held Joshua's hand in a tight grip. Then she picked up an afghan she had crocheted, walked him to the sofa, and wrapped the afghan around both of them. He snuggled close into her body, feeling warm and protected.

They stayed well away from the window, but over the top of the sofa, Joshua could see the sky.

"You see how beautiful that is?" his grandmother had asked. "When can you see a sky like that if not during a storm?"

As he grew older, Joshua lost his fear. When he was in the third grade, he tried to explain thunderstorms scientifically to his grandmother. She nodded at every word, but Joshua knew she didn't understand what he was saying.

He was amazed that Grandma Goldina didn't know anything about science. So he decided to teach her everything he had learned.

One Friday afternoon, while he was polishing the candlesticks, he asked her, "Did you know that caterpillars turn into butterflies?"

"If you say so," Grandma Goldina agreed.

"And tadpoles turn into frogs," he went on. "That's called metamorphosis," he added importantly.

Grandma Goldina was impressed. "Imagine what goes on in nature," she exclaimed.

The following Friday he brought a magnet.

"Today we'll talk about magnets," he announced, sounding just like his teacher, Miss Prince. "Give me a nail, Grandma."

"So go find a nail when you need one," she grumbled as she poked through her odds-and-ends box. "It has to be a nail? It can't be a needle?"

Joshua took the box to the kitchen table. He found some buttons, a pencil sharpened down almost to the eraser, three tacks, five paper clips, a broken rubber band, and a glue stick that was all dried out.

There were many other bits and pieces in the box, but Joshua didn't need them for the experiment. He handed his grandmother the magnet.

"See what you can pick up with the magnet," he ordered.

Grandma Goldina gave Joshua a small sideways glance. He thought she was smiling as she tried to pick up the rubber band with the magnet, but he wasn't sure.

"Try again," Joshua urged.

So she used the magnet on the pencil. Then she said gravely, "It doesn't work."

Before Joshua could say anything, however, she quickly moved the magnet over the paper clips, then to the tacks.

"You knew about magnets all the time," Joshua accused.

"My mother gave me a magnet a long time ago to pick up pins and my needle when I sewed." When she saw how disappointed he looked, she added, "I know it comes in handy, but why it works, and how it works, that you'll have to tell me."

So Joshua eagerly explained about the magnetic

47

forces that pulled and pushed things made of iron. When he spoke of positive poles and negative poles, Grandma Goldina leaned her head back and dozed off.

11

Joshua was glad it was raining today, because this would be a good time to talk to his grandmother about the planets. The class had learned all about the solar system this past week, and Joshua was bursting with information.

"Come on, Grandma," he called. "Today I'm going to teach you about the planets."

She called back from the kitchen. "The planets can wait, but not the dishes."

"She'll never get done," Joshua grumbled to himself. So, to pass the time, he dipped into the remembering box, pulling things out and putting them back, his mind still intent on the planets.

But when Grandma Goldina finally joined him on the sofa, he was holding a long, thick sock in his hand.

"Grandma, why would you save one old sock?"

49

"Look at that!" she exclaimed happily. "You found my old *knippel.* I forgot it was in the box."

"What's a *knippel?*" Joshua pronounced it the way his grandmother had, sounding the k: kuh-NIP-uhl.

Grandma Goldina settled back into a more comfortable position.

"When I came to America," she began, "I couldn't speak the language. Fresh off the boat, I was afraid of my own shadow. I never took one step away from my neighborhood on the East Side in New York, where I lived with a cousin. Later, of course, I met your Grandpa Abba."

"What about the sock?" Joshua hurried her.

But Grandma Goldina could never be hurried.

"He was a presser in a pants factory. I had a job sewing hair on dolls. When we got married, we didn't have enough money for furniture. In the kitchen, we had a table, but no chairs."

"You had to have chairs," Joshua argued. "What else could you sit on?"

"Boxes," his grandmother answered promptly. "I went to the vegetable man and he gave me two crates, orange crates. They were so ugly, I wanted to cover them, but I didn't have enough money to buy material. So I took a skirt I brought from the old country . . ." Grandma Goldina stopped talking for a moment, and that look was back on her face.

"You took a skirt," Joshua prompted, "and then what?"

"Was that a beautiful skirt! A beautiful pale blue, with a thin white stripe running through it. I cut it up and covered the crates with it. I even had enough material to make a little ruffle around the tops."

Joshua thought about the skirts his mother wore. Then he shook his head. "Grandma, you couldn't have. Not with one skirt —"

She held up her hand. "You're talking skirts in 1942. I'm talking skirts in 1892. In those days my skirts were so long, I had to hold them up when I went outside. Otherwise I would be sweeping the sidewalks with them."

She reached over and tapped Joshua on the tip of his nose. "Never mind the skirts. That I had. And orange crates I had. But what I wanted most in the world was a chair for your Grandpa Abba and a chair for me."

"Why didn't you just buy them?"

His grandmother shook a finger at him. "You're not listening. To buy something you first need money. We had to buy food and clothes and pay the rent. Everything else was a luxury. But we pinched a penny here from the food and a penny there from the clothes, maybe sometimes a nickel. Once, I remember, your Grandpa Abba found a dime in the street. A whole dime! It all went into the sock."

Joshua couldn't understand. "Why didn't you just put it in a little bank like the one I have?"

Joshua's bank was shaped like a dog. When he

pressed the dog's tail, a long tongue came out of its mouth. Then Joshua put a dime or a quarter on the tongue, and the tongue pulled it back into the dog's mouth.

Grandma Goldina had given Joshua the bank on his sixth birthday and had dropped a shiny new penny in Joshua's hand. "To give you a start," she explained.

Joshua wanted a bike, but he knew the only way he could have one was to save up for it. So on afternoons when he didn't have homework, or on Sundays, Joshua stayed close to the telephone booths in the drugstore on the corner. Most of the people on his block didn't own a phone. The pharmacist allowed them to get calls in the booths. Whenever a call came through, Joshua would race along the street and get the person to come to the phone. Sometimes he made as much as twenty or thirty cents a day!

Joshua realized suddenly that Grandma Goldina had stopped talking. She was looking at him fondly.

"See," she said. "Even a nine-year-old boy has things to remember."

12

"You still haven't told me why you didn't use a little bank, like the one you gave me," Joshua reminded his grandmother.

She shook her head. "And you're not paying attention. Even little banks cost money. When you're poor, you don't spend money to save money, you understand? Later, when things were a little easier for us, Grandpa Abba bought me a bank. I thought it was such an extravagance, but I loved it, because it looked like the Statue of Liberty. The Statue of Liberty was the first thing we saw when we came to America."

Joshua waved the sock in the air.

"Grandma, did everybody keep their money in socks?"

"Not exactly." She leaned back, trying to find the right words to explain how she and the people around her lived long ago.

"Listen, Joshua. In the olden days, even if she worked, a woman didn't have money of her own. Whatever she earned she had to turn over to her husband. Then he would give her enough money to buy food. That was called 'table money.' If she wanted money of her own, she would save what she could from the table money, put it in the middle of a handkerchief, and tie it into a knot. That knot was called a *knippel*. Do you understand what I'm saying?"

When Joshua nodded, she continued, "And then the woman would pin the *knippel* inside her dress where it would be hidden. That was her nest egg, her bank, her hope — "

"Mommy doesn't have a *knippel*," Joshua interrupted.

"I'm glad to hear it. This is a whole different world. But in those days, that's how it was. Except your Grandpa Abba never liked the idea. 'Whatever we save, we'll save together,' he always told me. 'No secrets.' So when we could, we untied the knot and put our pennies into the sock together. You wouldn't believe how long it took us to save two dollars. The secondhand man was saving two chairs for us, one dollar for each chair. A fortune, believe me."

"So then you got the chairs," Joshua said.

She shook her head. "No. I didn't. Because when I went to open the *knippel*, the money wasn't there."

Joshua was shocked. "Somebody stole your *chair* money?"

"That's what I thought. I couldn't wait for your Grandpa Abba to come home. 'Calm yourself, Goldina,' he told me. 'You weren't robbed. I took the money and gave it to Herschel Farber.' "

"But Grandma," Joshua protested, "you said you and Grandpa didn't have any secrets —"

"My words exactly," Grandma Goldina interrupted. " 'What happened to the no secrets?' I asked him. So he said, 'I couldn't tell you, Goldina. You weren't home. And even if you were there, I know how you feel about Herschel. He swore he didn't have food for his family for Shabbat. So what could I do? After all, he's a next-door neighbor.' "

"That's awful. How can you have Shabbat without food?" Joshua exclaimed.

"I gave your Grandpa Abba a terrible look," Grandma Goldina went on. " 'That gonif, that thief,' I said. 'When does Herschel Farber have money for anything? You know and I know that Herschel Farber is the world's biggest liar.'

"I started to cry," Grandma Goldina admitted. " 'Goodbye chairs,' I yelled at him. 'Goodbye money. Herschel Farber knows how to borrow, but not how to pay back.' Your Grandpa Abba took my hand in his. 'What could I do?' he asked me. 'Maybe just this once Herschel did need money for Shabbat. How could I say no?' Your grandfather could never say no," she added softly.

"So you never got your chairs." Joshua sounded sad.

"Of course I got my chairs," his grandmother said briskly. "I pawned my wedding ring."

"But you're wearing it," Joshua pointed out.

She looked down at her finger and spun the ring around. "Oh, your Grandpa Abba got it back for me. I knew he would." She had a pleased smile on her face, remembering. "That no-good Herschel Farber did two good things for us by taking my *knippel* money. To get my ring back for me, your Grandpa Abba decided to go to school and become a real American, with an education, so he could get a good job and make a good living. 'No more *knippels,*' he told me."

Grandma Goldina stopped talking, just sat quietly on the sofa, her hands folded in her lap.

Joshua waited a few minutes. Then he nudged her. "What was the second good thing Herschel Farber did, Grandma?"

"He gave us a present that lasted all our lives."

"Like what, Grandma? What kind of present can last that long?"

"Dig down into the sock, Joshua. Do you feel something there?"

Joshua pushed his hand clear down into the toe of the sock. When he pulled his hand out, he was holding two small torn pieces of cardboard with printing on one side and numbers on the other.

"Half of two movie tickets?" Joshua thought that

57

was peculiar. "Why would anybody save torn movie tickets?"

Grandma Goldina reached over and took them from his hand. "Not movie tickets. We didn't have movies in those days."

"Well, I guess you listened to the radio a lot, like we do."

"Radio?" Grandma Goldina repeated, laughing. "We didn't even have electricity. But we did have the theater, and what Herschel Farber gave us was two tickets to a play."

"But Grandma," Joshua objected, "where did he get money to buy tickets if he didn't have money for Shabbat?"

"See how smart you are!" Grandma Goldina exclaimed. "That man never paid for anything in his life. Always someone was sorry for him — poor Herschel, everybody called him. His cousin was supposed to go to the show, but he got sick. So Herschel coaxed him for the tickets. Then he went to your Grandpa Abba and gave him the tickets and explained this was how he was paying back the two dollars. I was so mad! 'I want my chairs,' I yelled at him, 'not pieces of cardboard.' But your Grandpa Abba insisted that we go to the theater."

Grandma Goldina smoothed the tickets gently. "What Herschel Farber gave us was magic. We laughed. We cried. For three hours those people on the stage made us live in another world. After that night, Grandpa Abba and I went to the theater whenever we could scrape the money together. And the wonderful thing was, Joshua, that the magic was always there."

Joshua could tell his grandmother was back in that world again, for she had her faraway look. He took the torn tickets from her hand, stuffed them carefully into the toe of the sock, and put the sock back into the remembering box.

"We're putting on a play in school about Christopher Columbus," he told her. "And I'm going to be Columbus because I have a good memory, my teacher says. I hardly ever forget a line."

"Christopher Columbus, *hoo-hoo!* Imagine," his grandmother said, sounding very impressed.

"And I get to discover America," Joshua went on.

"Why not?" she answered, smiling. "Didn't I also discover America?"

13

And so the Sabbaths came and went, and it was almost time for Joshua's tenth birthday.

"You'll be a man before I know it," Grandma Goldina told him. "Soon you'll be too grown up to come here for Shabbat."

"I'll never stop coming," Joshua said. "Even when I'm in college. I promise."

As it turned out, however, Joshua missed the next four Sabbaths. First all the Beck children came down with the flu. Then Grandma Goldina developed a cold she couldn't shake off.

On the fifth Sabbath, Joshua rang the bell on Friday afternoon as usual.

"You grew," Grandma Goldina marveled when she opened the door. "Look how you grew in just five weeks. Soon you'll be as big as my grandfather Schmuel."

"I didn't grow, Grandma. But I think you got

smaller." His grandmother seemed tinier and more frail than he remembered.

"Of course I'm smaller," she agreed at once. "When you get old, you shrink." She gazed at him fondly. "So, you think you still remember how to polish the candlesticks?"

"Do you still remember how to tell stories from the remembering box?" he teased.

"Now that you're almost ten years old, Joshua, it's time for you to have your own remembering box. Come. I'll show you."

Joshua followed his grandmother into the living room. He noticed that she had already put the white tablecloth on the table. He could smell the challah, which had just come from the oven. Then, next to the sofa, he saw a box that looked just like his grandmother's remembering box.

It, too, was a trunk, with two long straps around it. But it was much smaller than Grandma Goldina's box, and the lock worked.

While his grandmother leaned back on the sofa, Joshua sank to his knees to open the lid of the trunk.

"It's got some things in it." Joshua was surprised.

"Of course it has things in it. What kind of a present is an empty box?" she asked.

Joshua started to pull the items out one by one. "Hey! Here's your grandfather Schmuel's willow stick. And two blue ribbons. Are these the ribbons you tied on Mazel?"

Grandma Goldina nodded. "I want you to save them for me. Then you can make sure I wear them at your wedding."

"And your *knippel*! Why did you give me the *knippel*?" Joshua was puzzled.

"To remind you, when you grow up, that life is full of surprises."

But Joshua had already put the *knippel* back in the box because something else had caught his eye.

"What's this bell, Grandma? You never told me anything about this bell."

He examined it carefully, turning it round and

round, running his finger over the designs in the silver.

Grandma Goldina beamed. "When I was a little girl . . ." she began.

Joshua sat back expectantly. He hadn't heard a story about the old country for five long weeks.

His grandmother reached over and patted his head lovingly.

"When I was a little girl," she said again, "we lived in a little wooden house. All up and down our street were little wooden houses. We practically lived in each other's pockets we were so close together. Everyone lived that way. The streets were just dirt roads. The people were just able to scratch out a living. But when Shabbat came, it was like a touch of magic."

"Like when Herschel Farber gave you the theater tickets," Joshua interrupted.

"No. This was an altogether different kind of magic. This magic happened once a week. Inside each house, the women scrubbed and polished. White cloths were put on the tables. The freshly baked challahs gave off such a delicious fragrance . . ." She sniffed. "I can still smell them. It was better than perfume."

Joshua hid a smile. Grandma Goldina was smelling the challah on the table, right here in the room.

She didn't notice and went on with her story. "Soon Shabbat candles burned in every window.

And do you know how we knew when to light the candles?"

"You waited until the sun was going down."

"No. We waited for the bell ringer. He would walk up and down the streets, very slowly, swinging his bell back and forth, back and forth."

"Like this?" Joshua asked. He swung the little silver bell and listened as it tinkled quietly. "How could anybody hear that?"

"No, no, Joshua. He didn't have a bell like this. Let me tell you what happened."

Joshua sat up, wrapping his arms around his knees, squirming into a more comfortable position. Grandma Goldina was finally getting to the story about the silver bell.

14

"My uncle Hayim was the bell ringer. He had a big, old rusty bell that was loud but had no music. He went to my grandfather Shimon and complained. 'A bell for Shabbat should sing. Make me a bell that sings.' So my grandfather Shimon said, 'Why not? What else do we have?' And he made a bell that was so beautiful people came from other villages to see and hear it."

"Like this one?" Joshua asked, examining the bell once more.

"Just like this one. Only bigger. And with more designs. See?" She pointed to each one in turn. "Here is the lion lying down with the lamb. This is the burning bush. You remember Moses and the burning bush?"

"Of course. And I know this one, too. It's the dove of peace. And these are the hands of blessing."

"That was all he could get on the little bell," Grandma Goldina explained. "But on the big bell he gave to my uncle Hayim, he also carved the tree of life, the menorah, the Eternal Light, and the shofar. You know what the shofar is?"

"Grandma," he said, reproachfully. "I've known about the shofar all my life. It's the ram's horn that they blow on the High Holy Days in the synagogue."

Grandma Goldina laughed.

"You were just teasing me," he said. "You knew that I knew. Even Shoshanah knows, and she isn't even six years old yet.

"How come he made this bell for you?" Joshua asked. He was running his fingers over the raised designs again.

"He made it because I followed my uncle Hayim around, clapping a spoon against a dish. I wanted to be a bell ringer, too."

"Were you very little, Grandma?"

"I was five years old —"

"When was that?" Joshua was curious.

"That was in 1873."

"Grandma!" Joshua cried.

"Don't say it," his grandmother begged. "I know how old I am. Do you want to hear about the bell, or not?" When Joshua nodded, she rushed on. "My grandfather Shimon made the bell for me when he made the big one for my uncle Hayim. After that, when he walked through the village with

67

his new singing bell, I walked right behind him with my bell."

"Is that all he did, just ring the bell?" Joshua wanted to know.

"Of course not. He would also sing. '*Vibeles. Vibeles.* Little wives. Little wives. Sabbath approaches. Sabbath approaches.' I also wanted to sing something. So I called out the first words that popped into my head. 'Awake and sing,' I said. 'Awake and sing.' And one by one we could see the candles start to glow in the windows."

"I wish we had bell ringers," Joshua said wistfully. "Instead of looking at the calendar for the right time to light the candles." That reminded him. "Grandma! We forgot! We have to get everything ready."

"One more thing I have for you, then we'll get started." She reached into the pocket of her apron, then handed him a picture.

"Grandma! This is the picture I wanted. How come you're giving it to me now?" He glanced down at the twelve-year-old girl, her hair braided and tied with ribbons, and with a grin so broad dimples showed in her cheeks.

"It's time for you to have it. For your remembering box." Her voice was low; her eyes looked beyond him to another time. Then she closed her eyes and put her head against the back cushion.

"All of a sudden, I'm a little tired," she murmured. "Just let me rest a minute."

68

"Grandma," Joshua said after a while, "we have to get ready. It's getting dark."

She didn't answer.

He stared at the silver bell. Smiling, he swung it back and forth.

"Awake and sing, Grandma," he called. "Awake and sing."

But his grandmother did not awake.

"Grandma, please. You have to light the candles."

She did not move.

Joshua stared at her for a long moment. Then he went into the kitchen. Picking up the candlesticks, he brought them back into the living room and put them carefully on the table. He placed the candles in the candlesticks, bowed his head, and recited the blessing.

Finally he lit a match and touched the flame to the candlewicks. The light from the candles glowed softly, sending flickering shadows across Grandma Goldina's still face.

"Shabbat Shalom, Grandma," Joshua whispered. Then he went into the kitchen to phone his father.